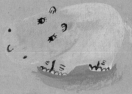

Ruby
AND THE NOISY HIPPO

To Sarah and
Laurel and Hardy
under the bed

KINGFISHER
Larousse Kingfisher Chambers Inc.
95 Madison Avenue
New York, New York 10016

First published in 2000
2 4 6 8 10 9 7 5 3 1
1TR/1199/TWP/HBM(HBM)/150NMA

LIBRARY OF CONGRESS CATALOGING-IN-PUBLICATION DATA
Stephens, Helen, 1972—
Ruby and the noisy hippo/wirtten and illustrated by Helen Stephens. —1st ed.
p. cm.
Summary: Noisy Hippo is so loud that Ruby does not want him to accompany her to the
candy store, but when his loudness saves her from a monster she decides that sometimes
it is okay to be noisy.

ISBN 0-7534-5226-X

[1. Hippopotamus—Fiction. 2. Noise—Fiction. 3. Monsters—Fiction.] I. Title.
PZ7. S83213 Ru 2000
[E] —dc21   99-049923
Printed in Singapore

Ruby and the NOISY HIPPO

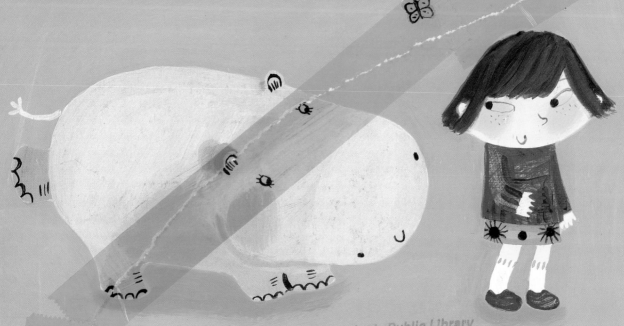

Helen Stephens

KINGFISHER

NEW YORK

"What is that horrible noise?" said Ruby.

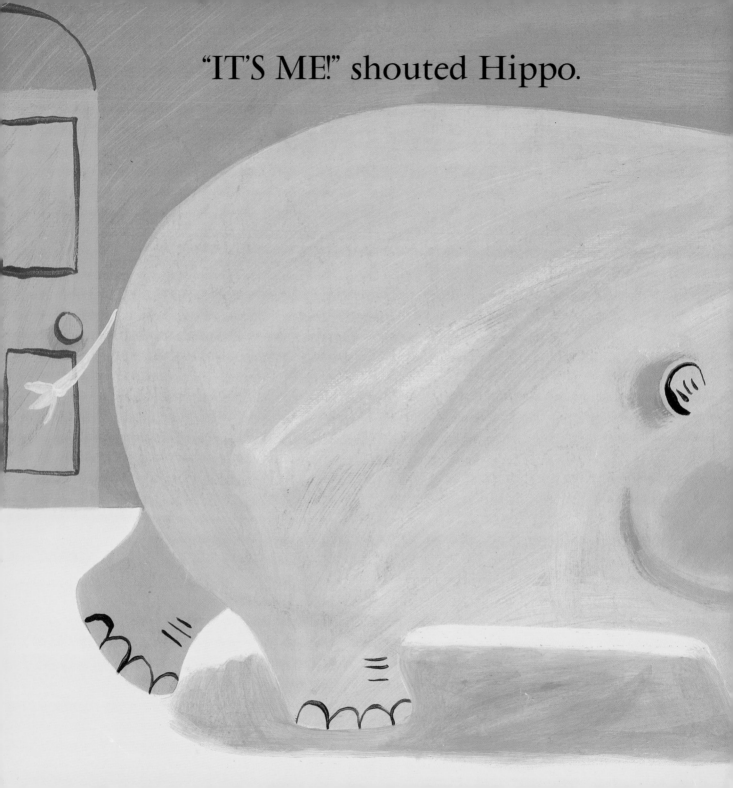

"IT'S ME!" shouted Hippo.

"May I come to the candy store with you?"

"Well . . . only if you promise to be very quiet," said Ruby, "or people will stare!"

"I promise," whispered Hippo.

And he was very quiet. For a little while . . . .

But by the time they reached the mailbox, Hippo was singing.
"Be quiet!" said Ruby. "You promised!"

By the time they reached the telephone booth, Hippo was singing at the top of his voice.

La
La!
La!
La!

By the time they reached the bus stop,
Hippo was singing and stomping his feet.

"That's it!" said Ruby. "You're too noisy. People are staring. You can't come to the candy store with me!"

Bang!
Bang!
Bang!

"Poor me," whispered Hippo.

Then he had an idea.

Hippo followed Ruby secretly . . .

all the way to the candy store.

"One bag of strawberry fizz
bombs, please," said Ruby.

closed

Then she went outside with her candy.

Suddenly, a great big candy-eating monster jumped out at Ruby. "Give me your strawberry fizz bombs!" he shouted.

Ruby was scared. Too scared to move.
Too scared to make a sound.

Bang! Bang!

Hippo stomped out of the bushes.
"LEAVE MY FRIEND ALONE!"

Bang!

The monster ran home crying.

"Thank you, Hippo," said Ruby.
"Maybe it's okay to be noisy sometimes."

Then Ruby and Hippo walked home together, singing and stomping their feet.